Let's Play Ball

By: Marty Allen
Illustrated by: Judann Weichselbraun

Copyrights and Permissions Departmen
Let's Play Bal
5662 Calle Real #18
Goleta, CA 9311

Library of Congress Cataloging in Publicatio
Dat
Allen, Mart
Let's Play Bal
Summary: A childs' first book. A little boy and his favorite past time playing bal
He experiences the balls as they relate to different sports or events in life
Original paintings done in watercolo
Graphic Design by Brown Design, Santa Barbara, CA

Library of Congress Card catalog 99-95275. ISBN 0-9672972-0-

Dedicated
to David Allen

I kick my soccer ball.

I pitch my baseball.

I catch my football.

I slap my volleyball.

I tee up my golf ball.

I swing at my tennis ball.

I bounce on my water ball.

I whack at my paddle ball.

HAWAI

I roll my bowling ball.

I push my big ball.

I shoot my basketball.

I rescue my beach ball.

Where is my little rubber ball?

I love them all!